GW00985778

Little Krishna

Harish Johari

with Sapna Johari

ILLUSTRATED BY PIETER WELTEVREDE

WITH SURESH JOHARI

Story adapted by Eliza Thomas

Bear Cub Books
Rochester, Vermont

For Dada Harish Johari

Special thanks to Vatsala Sperling
for all her expert help.

Bear Cub Books
One Park Street
Rochester, Vermont 05767
www.InnerTraditions.com

Bear Cub Books is a division of Inner Traditions International

LIBRARY OF CONGRESS CATALOGING-IN-PUBLICATION DATA

Johari, Harish, 1934-1999.
Little Krishna / Harish Johari with Sapna Johari ; illustrated by
Pieter Weltevrede with Suresh Johari; story adapted by Eliza Thomas.
p. cm.
Summary: Relates adventures of the young Krishna, the Hindu god who was
known as a child for his mischievous nature.
ISBN 1-59143-001-1
1. Krishna (Hindu deity)—Childhood—Juvenile literature.
2. Mythology, Hindu—Juvenile literature. [1. Krishna (Hindu deity).
2. Mythology, Hindu.] I. Johari, Sapna. II. Johari, Suresh, 1942–2000.
III. Weltevrede, Pieter, ill. IV. Thomas, Eliza. V. Title.
BL1220 .J6 2002
294.5'2113—dc21
2002008844

Printed and bound in China

10 9 8 7 6 5 4 3 2 1

This book was typeset in Berkeley
with Barbara Svelte and Fine Hand
as the display typefaces
Text design by Mary Anne Hurhula
Layout by Virginia Scott Bowman

People who practice Hinduism believe that Lord Krishna appeared on Earth thousands of years ago at a time when the powers of evil held the world in their terrible grip and demons swarmed over the land. Krishna was sent to Earth as the incarnation of Vishnu, God of Preservation, to save the world from destruction.

But nobody could save the world alone—not even the great Lord Vishnu. When he came to Earth as Krishna, he brought along a whole team of other gods and holy beings to help him restore order and beauty to the land. His serpent, Shesha, was born as the boy Balram. His wife, the goddess Lakshmi, came to earth as Krishna's beloved Radha, a simple milkmaid. Krishna's parents, friends, and cowherding companions had all been saints and sages in former lives.

Even though Krishna had a big job to do on Earth, he found time to be a real little boy who played pranks and made mischief and had a lot of fun. And no matter how naughty Krishna was, his mother, Yashoda, loved him with all her heart, as only a mother can. Krishna and his mother remind us that when children get all the love they need, they grow up strong and brave and ready to save the world. This story of Krishna's boyhood has been adapted from one of the sacred Hindu texts, the Bhagvad Purana.

Cast of Characters

Kansa, ('Kahn-sa) king of the demons, usurper of the throne of Mathura

Bhumi, ('Boo-mee) Earth goddess

Brahma, (Brahm-'ha) God of Creation

Vishnu, ('Vish-noo) God of Preservation, born on Earth as **Krishna** ('Krish-na)

Shesha, ('Shay-sha) Vishnu's serpent, born on Earth as **Balram** ('Bahl-ram)

Lakshmi, ('Lock-shmee) Vishnu's wife, born on Earth as the milkmaid **Radha** ('Rod-ha)

Devaki, (Day-vah-'kee) Kansa's sister and birthmother of Krishna

Vasudeva, (Vah-soo-'day-vah) Devaki's husband

Yogmaya, (Yohg-'my-a) Goddess of Illusion, born on Earth as a baby girl who changes into the goddess **Durga** ('Door-ga)

Rohini, (Ro-'hee-nee) mother of Balram

Ugrasena, ('Oog-rah-say-na) Kansa's father, the rightful king of Mathura

Saint Narada, ('Nah-rah-da) a holy spirit

Yashoda, (Yah-'sho-da) adoptive mother of Krishna, birthmother of Yogmaya

Nanda, ('Nahn-da) Yashoda's husband, adoptive father of Krishna

Trinavrata, (Trin-'ah-vra-ta) a demon who takes the form of a tornado

Prabhavati, (Prahb-'ha-va-tee) a milkmaid who grows weary of Krishna's pranks

Vatasura, (Vah-'tah-soor-a) a demon who takes the form of a calf

Bakasura, (Bock-'ah-soor-a) a demon who takes the form of a giant crane

Aghasura, (Agh-'ha-soor-a) a demon who takes the form of an enormous snake

Indra, ('In-dra) Lord of Rain, a demigod

Keshisura, (Keh-'shee-soor-a) a demon who takes the form of a horse

Akrura, (Ah-'kroor-a) Kansa's cousin, a good and holy man

Once upon a time, long ago, the world was overrun by terrible demons. They disguised themselves in all shapes and sizes. Gigantic cobras would wrap themselves around whole villages, crushing everything within their coils; seething whirlwinds would blacken the skies; monstrous horses with pounding hooves would trample all who stood in their way.

Their leader was a ruthless king named Kansa, who sent them on deadly missions to enrich his own palace coffers. Kansa stopped at nothing. If it suited him, he would kill an innocent little child without a second thought. Mothers everywhere tried to hide their children to keep them safe. But it was almost impossible to hide from the awful king.

Even the Earth goddess, Bhumi, was unable to protect the land. She became desperate, her heart overflowing with sorrow. Finally, she sought the aid of the other gods. Taking her favorite form, that of a gentle cow, she traveled first to Brahma, God of Creation.

"The earth is growing darker every day," she told him. "What can we do?"

"Only Vishnu, Lord of Preservation, can restore light and order now," Brahma replied. "We must go at once."

Vishnu lived far in the heavens, in a place called Kshir-Sagar, which means "Ocean of Milk." When Bhumi and Brahma arrived, they found Vishnu resting upon the coils of his great serpent, Shesha. Lakshmi, his wife, sat at his side. He held sacred objects in his four hands: a lotus, a conch, a disk, and a club.

The gentle goddess turned to him with tears in her eyes. “All that is good and beautiful is being destroyed,” she cried. “Most gracious lord, we need all your powers of preservation! Save the earth from this evil!”

Vishnu listened carefully. Then he rose.

"A baby boy will be born," he said. "His name will be Krishna, and he will grow strong and beautiful. He will have many friends—my friends in heaven—to help him rid the world of these demons." Then he smiled at Bhumi. "Krishna will have divine power," he said, "for it is I who will be the baby boy."

Meanwhile, in the kingdom of Mathura, Kansa's beloved sister had just celebrated her wedding. Devaki was as unlike her brother as day is to night, lovely and goodhearted. She had chosen for her husband an honest and kind man named Vasudeva. After the wedding, Kansa drove the couple to their new home in his chariot. The horses galloped swiftly, while the newlyweds held hands and whispered words of love and joy. But just then, they were interrupted by a strange, deep voice from the sky.

"Kansa, you are a fool!" the voice shouted. "Your sister's eighth son will be the death of you!"

Kansa drew the horses up, leaped from the chariot, and yanked his sister to the ground. Devaki screamed as Kansa, his eyes bulging with rage, drew his sword. In desperation, Vasudeva grabbed his arm. "You are powerful and brave, Kansa," the good husband pleaded. "You cannot kill your own sister on her wedding day! I beg you, show mercy now and I promise to bring you every son born to her."

Kansa knew that Vasudeva would keep his word, and so he finally agreed to let the newlyweds go free. He smiled wickedly to himself. He was safe. He had already imprisoned his own father, the rightful king, Ugrasena. Surely no one would stand in his way. There was no need to kill his own sister, when he could so easily slaughter her eighth son.

When Vasudeva, as he had promised, brought Kansa their first baby, the king gave the baby back unharmed. After all, the prophecy had foretold that it would be the eighth boy who would kill him. Shortly after Vasudeva left, however, Kansa had another visitor. The spirit, Saint Narada, carried a lotus.

"Look!" he said. "Eight petals. Which is the first? Which is the eighth?"

Kansa fingered the petals thoughtfully. In the circle of the flower, any petal could be the first—or the eighth. Maybe this first baby boy might also be the eighth as well!

So the wicked king threw Devaki and Vasudeva into a dungeon. He wrenched the baby boy from his sister's arms and killed him. Year after year, Devaki gave birth to another son. Kansa murdered every one.

When Devaki found that she was pregnant a seventh time, she despaired, convinced that any child she bore was doomed. She did not know that this time the baby she carried was no ordinary mortal—or that the gods already had a plan to save him from Kansa's clutches.

Vishnu summoned the goddess Durga, who was also known as Yogmaya, Goddess of Illusion. She could change shape whenever she wanted and make people see whatever she wanted them to see.

"I need your help," said Vishnu. "Listen carefully. Devaki is pregnant with my companion Shesha, who will be born as Balram, a baby boy. We must move him from Devaki's womb before he is born. People will believe that Devaki had a miscarriage, but in fact another good mother in the palace, Rohini, will give birth to her baby. Then, I will enter Devaki's womb as Krishna."

Yogmaya spread a deep sleep over Devaki and Rohini and transferred the baby. Vishnu gave her more instructions.

"There is a loving couple in Gokul, just across the river. Their names are Nanda and Yashoda. On the same night that I am born as Krishna, you will be born to Yashoda as a little girl. Then we will switch places. Nanda and Yashoda will bring up Krishna as their own child. That way Kansa will never find him. Devaki will pretend that she gave birth to you as her own daughter. If Kansa gives her any trouble, show him who you really are. That should give him a good scare!"

When the August moon rose full in the sky, Devaki's eighth son was born. He first appeared haloed in a heavenly glow. Adorned with the ornaments of Vishnu, he held his sacred objects in his hands—the conch shell, lotus flower, disk, and club. His parents knew they were in God's presence and folded their hands in worship. Then Devaki grew afraid for the little boy's safety and begged the child to assume a mortal form.

The child spoke to her. "Dearest Mother, this is not the first time I come to earth. In this life I will be known as Krishna. Though I have a new name, I am always the same being—Lord Vishnu, himself."

After he spoke, the sacred objects vanished, and he looked like any other baby boy. The shackles that had bound Devaki and Vasudeva also snapped apart, and the locks on the door broke open.

"We must hide him," cried Devaki. "Quickly, before Kansa arrives!" They wrapped the little boy in blankets. Devaki sadly kissed her son good-bye, and Vasudeva fled with him from the dungeon.

Yogmaya had been busy casting her spell of slumber, and no one saw them escape. Outside, the skies had opened in torrential rain, but the serpent Shesha spread his great hoods over the baby to protect him from the downpour. The river roared and spilled from its banks, but the waters were quieted by one touch of the little baby's foot, and Vasudeva carried Krishna safely to the other side.

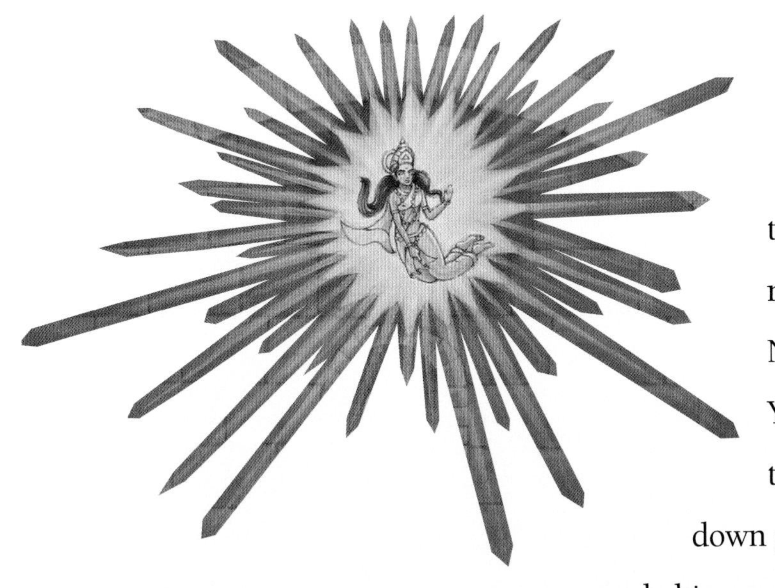

Vasudeva knew just what to do. He brought his newborn child to the house of Nanda and Yashoda, where Yashoda had just given birth to a baby girl. He laid his son down gently at Yashoda's side and made his way back to the prison carrying her little daughter in his arms.

Devaki welcomed the baby girl with open arms. A child to love, to cherish, to care for at last! Surely her brother would not kill a baby girl!

When Kansa heard of the birth, he stormed into the dungeon room. There he saw Devaki rocking her daughter, singing sweet lullabies. He snarled at her in anger. "Give her to me," he said.

"Dear brother, don't kill my baby," begged poor Devaki. "She is just a little girl. She will not harm you. Have mercy for once!" But Kansa roughly seized the baby.

"I will spare no child of yours!" he shouted and raised his arms to fling the newborn baby against the stones. "I'll smash her head!" he cried—but his hands were empty. Slipping effortlessly from his grasp, the baby had floated to the highest reaches of the room. In a burst of blinding light, the child revealed her true form—the fearsome goddess Durga.

"The boy who is to end your life has already been born," Durga said. "It is useless to murder more children."

Trembling, Kansa turned to Devaki and her husband. "I release you both," he said. "I will not harm you or your children, anymore." His voice shook as he turned away. "My sister will live freely, and without fear," he whispered to himself. "But what will become of me?"

On the other side of the river, Yashoda and her husband, Nanda, woke from a deep and forgetful sleep to find a baby boy lying at their side. Yashoda smiled. "I must have been dreaming," she said to Nanda. "I thought our baby was a girl. But look how beautiful our son is!"

Yashoda and Nanda delighted in their baby's growth.

"See how strong he is?" Yashoda said proudly. "He can roll over already, and he's only three months old!" Well, lots of babies roll over, but before long Yashoda's baby began to do some really extraordinary things. One day he kicked over a hundred-pound cart full of milk and yogurt.

Another day, as Yashoda was playing with him outside, he suddenly seemed to grow very heavy. Yashoda was used to carrying him on her hip, but soon the weight was too much for her. I must be more tired than I realized, she thought. She put the baby down and sang to him while she swept the porch. The dust blew in all directions as a gust of wind swirled around mother and baby. Another storm on the way, thought Yashoda.

She didn't know, of course, that Kansa's demons were scouring the land for Krishna and that the dust storm gathering over Gokul was in fact the demon Trinavrata. When the whirlwind scooped up her beloved son, she screamed.

Trinavrata carried Krishna high away inside the storm. Like Yashoda, the demon was surprised at the weight of this small baby. Krishna, smiling calmly, continued to grow heavier and heavier. Frantically, Trinavrata tried to drop the child, but Krishna held on tight, and together they tumbled from the sky. The demon's body was smashed to pieces on the ground; Krishna, still clutching his neck, was unharmed. Yashoda rejoiced. It seemed a miracle that he had survived such a fall. When she picked him up, he was as light as before, but she thought nothing of it.

As Krishna grew a little older, he and Balram played together constantly. They were the favorites of the village milkmaids, and their mothers doted on them proudly. Yashoda and Rohini dressed their young boys colorfully, Krishna in yellow with a crown of peacock feathers in his hair, and Balram in blue. The two boys ventured from the palace, making friends wherever they went—and sometimes getting into a lot of trouble!

One day, they were playing outside with a few of the other village boys, digging in the dirt, making mud pies, and getting very dirty. After a while one of the older boys ran to Yashoda. "Krishna has been bad!" he said. "Krishna has been eating clay!"

Yashoda was annoyed with her young son. "Did you really eat clay?" she demanded. "How many times have I told you not to put things in your mouth!"

Krishna didn't want to be punished, so he played a trick on Yashoda. "See, Mother? I haven't been eating anything." He opened his mouth wide.

Yashoda peered inside. There, in the little boy's mouth, she saw the whole universe—Earth and stars, the vast and empty spaces, the oceans and the mountains. Spirit, matter, cosmos, and fire—all were contained within. She realized then that Krishna was Lord Vishnu himself, and she was about to fall before him in worship.

But Krishna didn't want her to worship him. He just wanted her to love him the way mothers love their children all over the world. He could easily have come to Earth in his original form to fight the

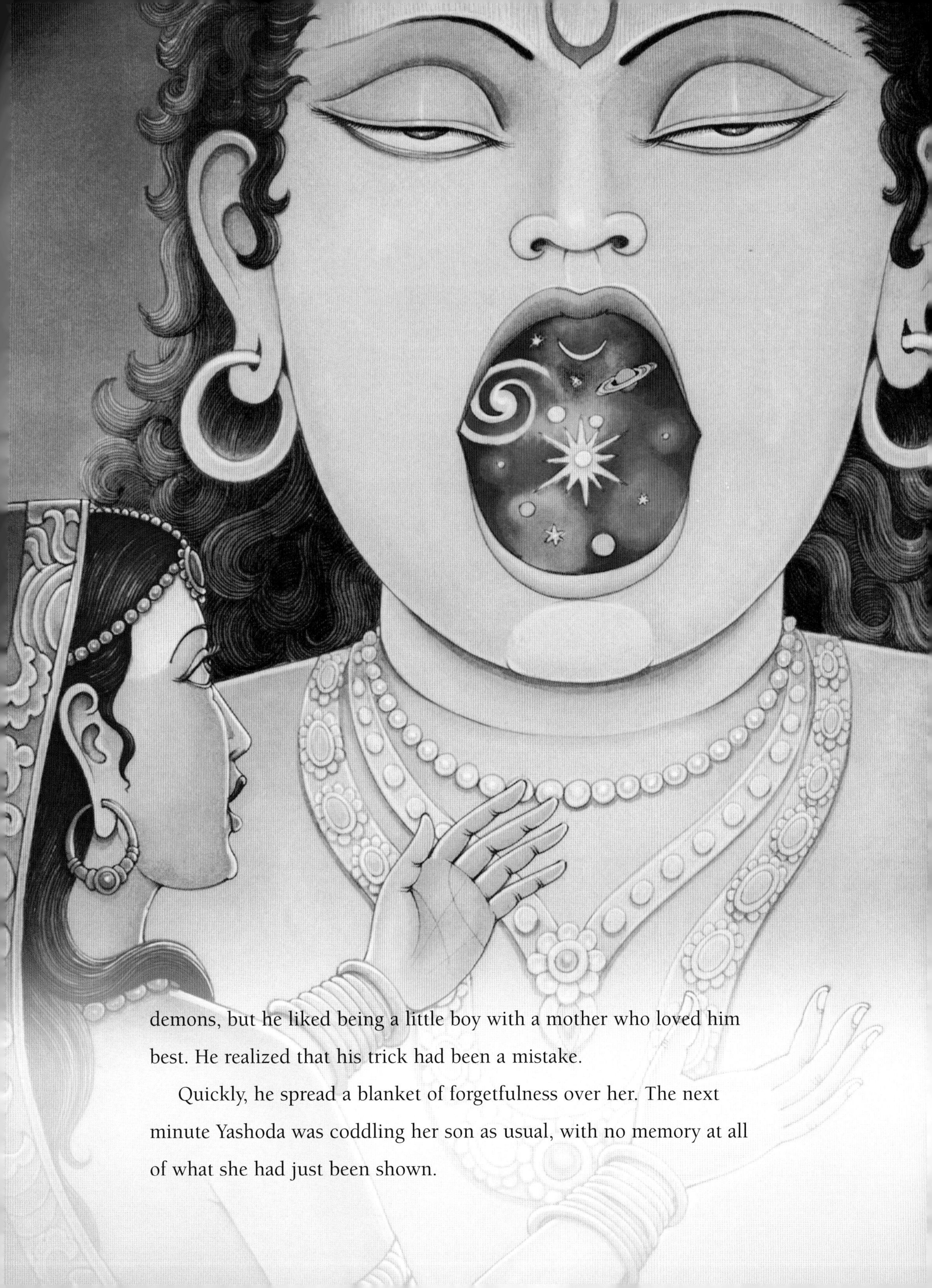

demons, but he liked being a little boy with a mother who loved him best. He realized that his trick had been a mistake.

Quickly, he spread a blanket of forgetfulness over her. The next minute Yashoda was coddling her son as usual, with no memory at all of what she had just been shown.

And so Krishna grew up as a mortal and made friends and played pranks. And caused his mother no end of trouble!

He was an agile and adventurous little boy, and Yashoda had a terrible time keeping up with him. He would run and hide under tables and stools. Then he began climbing on top of the tables and stools, grabbing butter from the hanging pots, giggling mischievously as he threw handfuls at the monkeys. Soon he started stealing butter and milk from his neighbors' houses as well. Krishna would often bring his friends along, and the group would distribute their loot among the poorer children of the village. (Kansa taxed these villagers harshly; many families had barely enough to eat, so there was more to Krishna's naughtiness than met the eye.)

The milkmaids recognized that there was something special about the boy and were charmed by his playful teasing. They would get up early and set aside pots of butter for Krishna to take and laugh at his antics. But one morning, a milkmaid named Prabhavati had had enough of the thefts and teasing. She caught Krishna red-handed as he was raiding her pot and giving handfuls of her butter to his friends. She marched him sternly back to Yashoda.

Krishna didn't want his mother to be angry with him, but he couldn't run away from Prabhavati. Just before they reached his mother, he disguised himself as Prabhavati's own son.

Prabhavati marched straight up to Yashoda."This boy of yours stole all my butter this morning!" she said angrily.

Yashoda began to laugh. "*My* boy?" she asked. "Then what is *your* boy doing here?"

Prabhavati looked down. Her own son looked up. Confused and embarrassed, the milkmaid left Yashoda's house. Outside the door, she looked down again. Krishna looked up. He grinned playfully.

"Watch out!" he teased. "Next time you interfere I'll turn myself into your husband!"

Astonished, Prabhavati dropped his hand and returned home. And now that they knew who he really was, no milkmaid dared to tangle with Krishna again.

But oh, did they ever complain. They came to Yashoda every day. They meant the boy no harm—they just enjoyed relating tales of his spirited mischief. Besides, they believed that the more complaints a child received, the longer the child would live, and so they understood that telling tales of his naughtiness would only bring him luck. What a litany of woes they had to offer!

"Yashoda, your child lets the cows go free at milking time!"

"Yashoda, he steals all my butter!"

"Yashoda, he is too smart! He runs away and we can't find him!"

"Yashoda, he and his friends break my best pots!"

"Yashoda, he and his friends snatch the milk and butter right off our heads when we go to market!"

"Yashoda, look at him! He is just pretending to be innocent!"

Yashoda would listen gravely. Then she would look down at her son's beautiful face. Even though she certainly knew of his many pranks, she would be overwhelmed with affection.

"You're a very, very naughty boy," she would say to him. But her voice was gentle, and her eyes shone with love.

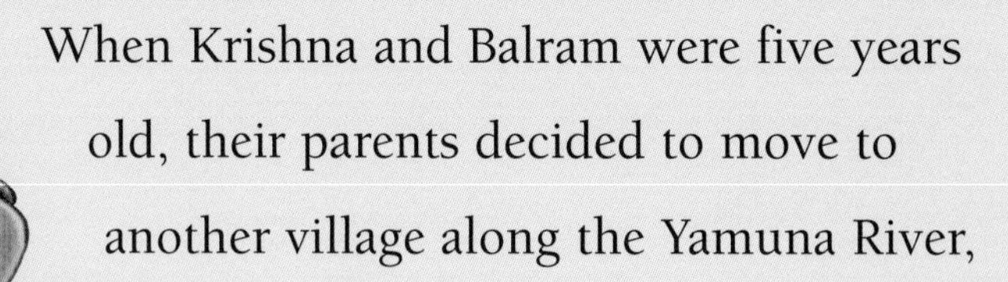

When Krishna and Balram were five years old, their parents decided to move to another village along the Yamuna River, hoping to escape the growing number of demons in Gokul. And so the households, along with all the cattle and servants and milkmaids, moved to Vrindavan. The countryside was lush and green, with lovely, rolling hills and wonderfully scented forests. The riverbanks sloped gently to the clear water. The boys were old enough now to tend the cows and calves and would happily spend their days outside with the herd.

Krishna had begun playing the flute. His music was truly divine, soothing the souls of all who heard it. Wild deer would come to listen, staring at him with their wide, glistening eyes. Peacocks would dance for him, and birds would flock to the heavenly sound of his melodies. The river itself would stop flowing, as if entranced to stillness. The leaves on the trees would cease fluttering, and soft clouds would gather to shield young Krishna from the heat of the sun. The cows especially loved Krishna and his flute and would stand alert, moving only their ears, as if they wanted to pour the sweet nectar of the music into their bodies.

One morning as Krishna played, a new calf sidled out of the woods and tried to join the herd. In truth, it wasn't a calf at all. It was Vatasura, one of Kansa's demons in disguise, and it had followed Krishna all the way to Vrindavan.

“I’ll kick him to death when he comes to pet me,” Vatasura said to himself. He lashed out with his pointed hooves when Krishna drew near, but the boy had seen through the disguise. Catching hold of the hind legs and tail, Krishna flung Vatasura high into a tree, killing him instantly.

The next demon arrived soon after. This one was named Bakasura and looked like an enormous crane with sharp talons and a long pointed beak.

"I will stab him to death with my long beak!" Bakasura said to himself. But Krishna ripped his beak apart as if it were a blade of grass.

Aghasura, the demon snake, was Bakasura's brother and far stronger and more cunning.

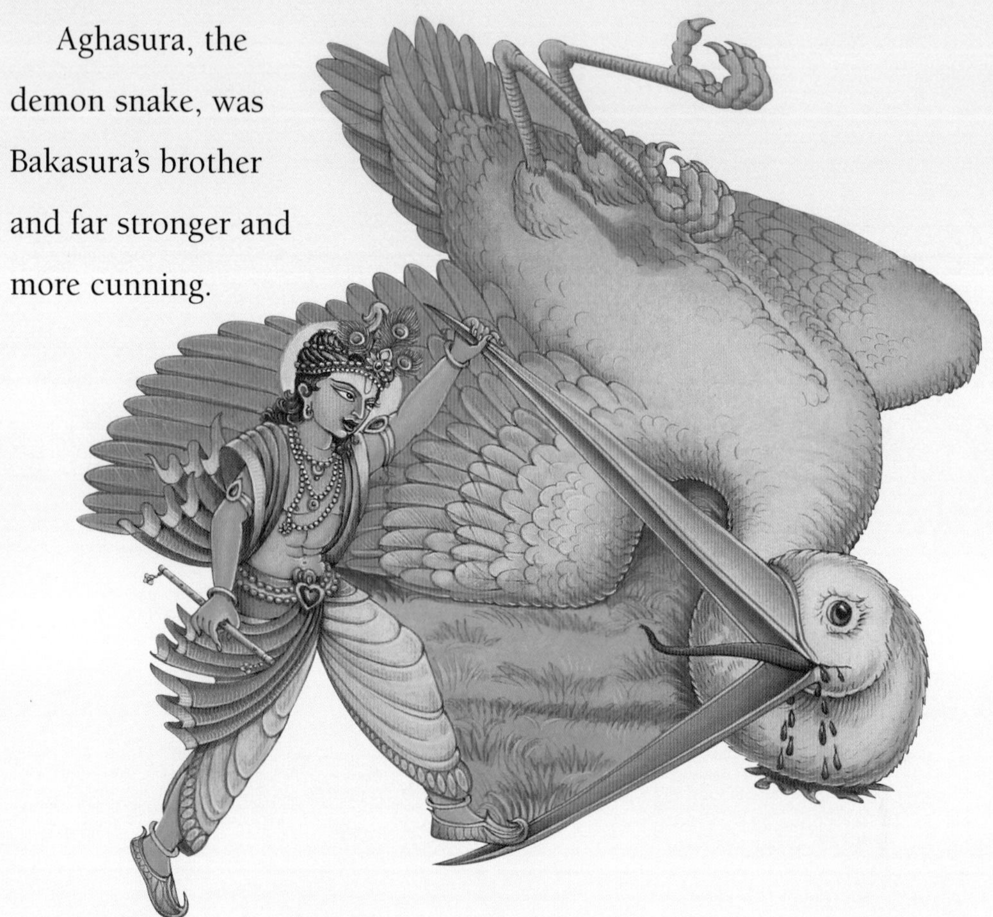

Opening his jaws wide, he waited for Krishna and the other cowherds to pass by.

"I will eat the boy alive," he said to himself.

Krishna entered the dark opening. He expanded his body inside the huge throat, pushing out against the sides. As Aghasura choked to death, his long body coiled and uncoiled, uprooting trees and bushes as far as the eye could see.

Krishna led his friends to the banks of the Yamuna River. "Let's stop here," said Krishna. "There is grass and cool water for the calves and a shady tree where we can have our lunch." The friends were relieved that one more demon was destroyed. They laughed and joked together as they sat down to eat.

It was awhile before they noticed that the herd had wandered off.

"They can't have gone far," Krishna said to the others. "I'll be right back with them." He called to the calves, going deeper and deeper into the surrounding forest and hills.

At that very moment Lord Brahma, happened to be looking down from heaven. He was surprised to see Krishna, acting like any ordinary boy, whistling for his lost calves. Brahma began to wonder. Was Krishna really the supreme god? Why wasn't he using his divine powers to search out the herd? And how could a supreme god lose his own cows, anyway? Brahma decided to test the young boy's powers. He cast a spell of slumber over the calves—and, for good measure, the boys as well—and hid them in a mountain cave.

Krishna continued calling and searching, but the calves were nowhere to be seen. Puzzled, he returned to the riverbank, only to find that his friends had disappeared as well. Krishna knew then that Brahma had stolen them all away.

"So," he thought, "Brahma has played a trick on me? I can play tricks, too!"

Instead of searching farther, Krishna simply created exact copies of every boy and every calf. When he returned to the village, he was surrounded by his companions, herding the calves as if nothing had happened. Mothers embraced their sons, and cows started licking their young. No one could tell the difference.

Brahma, when he next looked down to earth, was again surprised by what he saw. "Now what?" he thought. "The boys are still fast asleep in the cave. But there they are, dancing and singing with Krishna in the village. How can they all be in two places at the same time?"

Krishna saw that Brahma was watching again and played one last trick. He changed every boy again, this time into his own divine form, Vishnu. Each was illuminated with intense blue light, each was dressed in yellow garments, and each held the sacred conch, lotus flower, disk, and club. Brahma was overwhelmed. Tears streamed down his face.

"Forgive me for doubting your powers," he said. He folded his hands and bowed to Krishna. "Please, I am so sorry I interrupted your afternoon. Please, go back and have your lunch now."

Brahma returned the sleeping boys and calves to the banks of the Yamuna.

When the boys awoke, Krishna stood before them. They had no idea what had happened, or how much time had passed. "Good!" they said. "You found all the calves! Let's eat now." After the meal, Krishna played the flute as he led the children back to the village. He wore a peacock feather and forest flowers in his crown.

Krishna grew more handsome with each passing year. His hair was dark and curly, his limbs long and agile and lithe. His smile lit up the darkest day, while his eyes shone like the moon in the deep of night. When he danced, his body leaped and unfurled, as graceful as a leaf tossed in the lightest of breezes. The milkmaids, who had always been enchanted with the little boy, found themselves falling in love with him. Each maid wanted him for her husband.

They asked the goddess Durga for help and began a month-long fast in her honor. In the morning, the milkmaids would go to the river to bathe. After their swim, they would make an idol of sandalwood paste and flowers and pray for the goddess's blessing.

On the last day of the fast, Krishna happened to walk by the river where the young girls were bathing. They had left their clothes in a pile on the riverbank. Krishna gathered them all up and climbed into a tree. "Come and get them!" he called mischievously to the young girls. "I have all your clothes right here!"

"Beloved Krishna, please don't play tricks on us. We don't want you to see us naked. Give us back our clothes! We are cold!" The poor girls stood in the river, shivering.

"If you are so devoted to me," the young lord teased, "why don't you do as I ask?"

The milkmaids had no choice. One by one they left the cold water, covering themselves as best they could. Krishna gazed at them, one by one. The milkmaids were amazed to feel cleansed and fulfilled. Their longing for him turned to pious adoration.

Krishna was impressed by their simplicity and devotion. On a cool, moonlit evening he called them all to a beautiful spot by the Yamuna River.

"You know who I am," he said. "And I see that your love is pure and deeply spiritual. Tonight, I offer myself to each of you." After he spoke, his form multiplied, reappearing again and again, until each girl found herself standing with her own Lord Krishna. Krishna himself stood in the middle with Radha, the sweetest and loveliest among them. He took out his flute and began to play.

The milkmaids dipped and swirled, each with her own Krishna partner. They danced to the beautiful music late into the night.

Radha won the real Krishna's heart with her purity and beauty, and soon enough they were inseparable partners.

"As long as the sun and moon shine in the sky," Krishna sang to her, "your name shall be chanted with mine. And as long as the rivers flow on earth, our love will endure."

Near the end of the dry season, the men of Vrindavan prepared a ceremony in honor of Indra, the Lord of Rain. Nanda told Krishna that the ceremony was a family tradition. "When we need water for our crops," he explained, "we pray to Indra."

"But Indra is only a demigod," argued Krishna. "It will rain when the clouds have gathered enough water. Instead of flattering Indra, we should worship Goverdhan Hill, which overlooks our land."

He convinced Nanda to halt the preparations for Indra and gave directions for the new ceremony. The villagers prepared fragrant dishes and invited holy men to offer special prayers. They distributed food and clothing among the poor. At the end of the ceremonies Krishna accepted offerings for Goverdhan Hill. "All hills," he said, "are sacred. They offer protection from the wind and rain. They provide shelter for the animals."

Indra was furious. He sent dark clouds, unleashing torrents of water. Fierce winds whipped through the village, and the people feared for their lives. Krishna decided to teach the demigod a lesson. He picked up Goverdhan Hill on one finger and balanced it over the village like a big umbrella, gathering the inhabitants and all their livestock beneath. The winds howled and the rain poured, but the people and animals of Vrindavan stayed safe and dry.

After a week Indra called off the gales, and Krishna put the hill back in its place. People returned to their houses, and the livestock went back to the fields. Then Indra came down from the blue sky, riding Airawat the elephant and bringing with him Kamadhenu, the sacred cow of demigods. Humbled, he begged forgiveness.

Airawat showered holy water from heaven. Kamadhenu sprinkled Krishna with a soft rain of creamy milk and thanked him for shielding the livestock from the wrath of Indra. Ever since this time, Krishna has also been known as Govinda, the protector of Cows.

Kansa had sent demon after demon in his effort to locate and slay the eighth son of Devaki. One after another, Krishna destroyed them, and Kansa never learned of the boy's exact whereabouts.

Saint Narada knew that lasting peace was not possible unless the prophecy was fulfilled. It was time for Krishna to destroy the cruel king. To hasten the final confrontation, the holy spirit once again visited Kansa.

"Fool!" he said. "Don't you realize that Vasudeva and Devaki hid Krishna across the river the night he was born? Don't you know that Yashoda and Nanda, now living in Vrindavan, have brought up Krishna as their own son?"

Kansa was enraged and immediately put his sister and her husband in shackles. Then he summoned one of the most dangerous of all demons, a monstrous horse named Keshisura.

"Go to Vrindavan," he said. "Kill the boy."

Keshisura's demon hooves pounded, and his streaming mane hissed ominously in the wind when Krishna sped to meet him. The boy dodged the deadly hooves and threw the demon a hundred yards. Again Keshisura attacked, turning his fierce head to bite. Krishna stood his ground, plunging his arm down the throat of the beast. With a terrible scream, the horse fell to the ground. The cowherds grabbed sticks and ran to Krishna's aid, but Keshisura was already dead.

Kansa, hearing of Keshisura's death, set in motion a devilish plot. He called together the strongest fighters and the most experienced elephant trainers of the land.

"We will stage a wrestling match against Krishna and Balram," he said. "People will come far and wide to see such a great contest. As soon as the boys arrive, an elephant will attack them at the gate."

He turned to the group of wrestlers. "If the animal fails to kill them, the boys must die in the contest itself. Surely there are enough of you to defeat two boys!"

Then he called on his cousin Akrura. Because Akrura was a relative, Kansa took his allegiance for granted. Kansa told Akrura the details of his plot, adding that once Krishna and Balram were destroyed, he would also execute Devaki and her husband and then kill his father. No one would stand in his way!

"I have ordered a chariot. You will travel to Vrindavan and bring back the boys," he told his cousin. Akrura agreed to do as Kansa asked, but secretly he rejoiced that the prophecies might soon be fulfilled, for in truth, he despised the cruel king. He prayed that Kansa, not Krishna, would be the one to die.

Akrura arrived in Vrindavan the next evening. Krishna and Balram greeted him warmly. Akrura told the boys of Kansa's plot to kill them.

The two boys looked forward to fighting the king at last. "We are ready to leave tomorrow," they told Akrura. When Nanda heard of the contest, he declared he would accompany them. He would bring along his best sweet milk and yogurt as a victory prize.

"I'm not afraid," he told them. "You are strong and courageous, and I'm certain you will win."

But the people of Vrindavan were worried. The elders feared for Krishna's safety, and his younger friends were saddened that Krishna was leaving the village. Yashoda prayed endlessly for Krishna, pacing back and forth through the rooms of their house. And poor Radha was heartbroken that her beloved would soon be separated from her. How could she live without him? She grew feverish and distraught.

Krishna came to her house in the evening to comfort her. He would always be with her in her dreams, he said. He would come to her side every month, when the moon was full. Their love was pure and everlasting, he said. She must not lose herself in grief.

The next morning Krishna greeted everyone who gathered by Akrura's chariot. He thanked them for coming to see him off. "Don't worry, I will be back," he said.

But Radha was inconsolable. She lay in the path of the chariot, desperate to prevent him from leaving. Krishna went to her again.

"Sweet Radha, keep this as a token of my love," he said, giving her his beautiful flute. "Think of me when you hold it."

Radha smiled at him through her tears. "I will take good care of it while you are gone," she said.

At the banks of the Yamuna, Akrura drew up the chariot to give them all a chance to wash up and rest awhile. Akrura decided to take a short swim as well and dove out to the middle of the river. When he first looked back at the shore, Krishna and Balram were relaxing in the chariot. Akrura dove again under the cool water.

But when he raised his head to look once more, he saw something that made his whole body tingle with awe and wonder. Shimmering in midair over the water, Krishna sat cross-legged upon the coils of a mighty serpent. His eyes were shaped like lotus blossoms and shone with divine light. Adorned with jewels, he held in his four hands the sacred objects of Vishnu.

Akrura shivered. He bowed deeply. Then the vision was gone.

Back on shore, he rushed to the chariot to fall at Krishna's feet.

"What happened? Did you see something strange out there on the water?" Krishna asked him with a gently teasing smile.

Akrura raised his eyes. "I saw you," he said simply. Krishna embraced him, blessing the good man, and the three resumed their journey.

When they entered the city, crowds lined the streets in excitement. Everyone had heard about the wrestling match! Holy men gave them wreaths of flowers, and others offered fruits and sweets, clothes and jewels.

Early the next morning, the beating of drums announced the beginning of the contest. On a high podium overlooking the arena, Kansa watched the entrance gate. Would Krishna and Balram somehow survive the elephant attack he had planned? Would they crawl through the gate, bleeding and broken? Minutes ticked by. The boys were late. The attack must have been successful, Kansa thought. Surely Krishna and Balram were dead.

Then he heard the crowd gasp in awe. Far below, the two boys had entered into the arena. They walked with an elegant, effortless grace. Each boy balanced on his shoulder a shining elephant tusk.

Kansa felt his skin grow cold. Fear invaded his heart. The prophecy would be fulfilled.

This was a fight to the death, and the wrestlers didn't have a chance. Krishna and Balram, outnumbered manyfold, slew the first five; the others fled in disarray.

The king cried out in desperate rage. He ordered his guards to capture the boys. He ordered his soldiers to kill Devaki and Vasudeva. He shouted angrily for his own father to be put to death. But Krishna was already upon him. Brushing aside Kansa's sword, he threw the king into the arena, leaped upon him, and killed him with a single blow. When Kansa's eight brothers attacked, Balram and Krishna slew them as one. The battle was over.

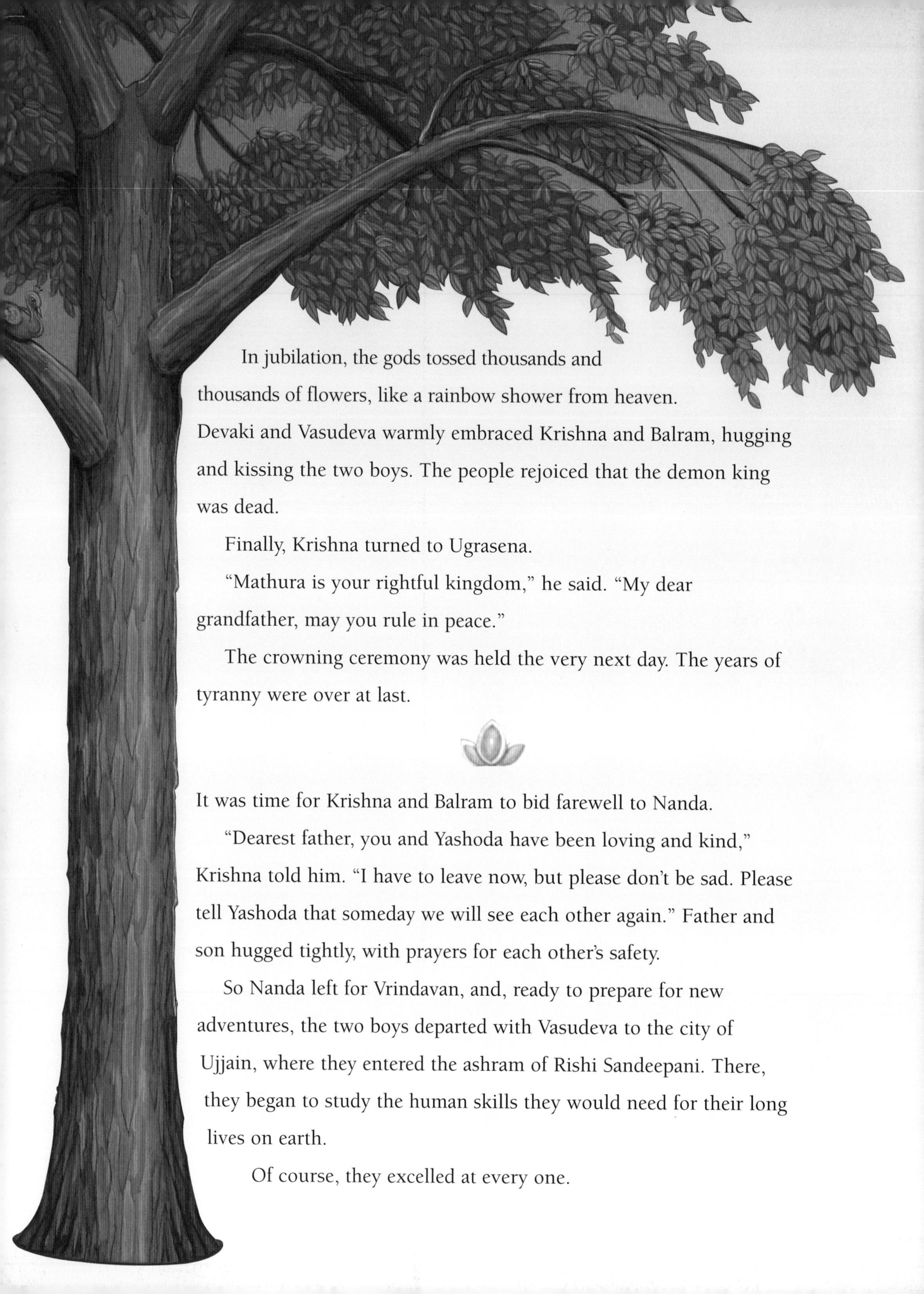

In jubilation, the gods tossed thousands and thousands of flowers, like a rainbow shower from heaven. Devaki and Vasudeva warmly embraced Krishna and Balram, hugging and kissing the two boys. The people rejoiced that the demon king was dead.

Finally, Krishna turned to Ugrasena.

"Mathura is your rightful kingdom," he said. "My dear grandfather, may you rule in peace."

The crowning ceremony was held the very next day. The years of tyranny were over at last.

It was time for Krishna and Balram to bid farewell to Nanda.

"Dearest father, you and Yashoda have been loving and kind," Krishna told him. "I have to leave now, but please don't be sad. Please tell Yashoda that someday we will see each other again." Father and son hugged tightly, with prayers for each other's safety.

So Nanda left for Vrindavan, and, ready to prepare for new adventures, the two boys departed with Vasudeva to the city of Ujjain, where they entered the ashram of Rishi Sandeepani. There, they began to study the human skills they would need for their long lives on earth.

Of course, they excelled at every one.

Note to Parents and Teachers

In India, parents tell children the story of Krishna's childhood not only to entertain them (though the story is quite entertaining), but also to teach them some important lessons about life. Krishna's universal message is as timely and meaningful for us today as it was when the story was written centuries ago in a far-off land.

The first lesson Krishna teaches is the importance of cooperation and teamwork. When Hindu gods incarnate in human form they do so to establish social order and justice. For instance, Vishnu needs a team of people with various strengths and skills to help him successfully restore order on Earth. No matter how powerful any given god is, a single god could never accomplish such a goal alone. When his heavenly cohorts accompany him to Earth as Balram, Radha, and Krishna's village playmates, they serve to illustrate this point.

When negative energies dominate the earth—in times of war, famine, or political repression—women and children often suffer the most. Under such circumstances, children are forced to grow up too fast. The repressive King Kansa kills children and sends demons out in search of Krishna. Nevertheless, secure in his mother Yashoda's love, Krishna remains a happy and playful child. He represents the irrepressible joy of being that should be every child's birthright. Krishna's childhood stories remind us that no matter how much the outer world threatens our children, we should do all we can to provide them with a safe and nurturing home where they can enjoy just being children.

Love, especially a mother's love for her child, is an important theme in Krishna's story. Though Krishna is really a god—Vishnu, God of Preservation—he doesn't want Yashoda to worship him with blind devotion in the way that people worship a divinity. Mothers in India try to see their children as potential divine beings, but every mother knows that what a real child needs is the expression of her love in action. She must simply love the child with all her heart, tend to its needs, and take every good care to protect it from harm.

Hindu theology defines nine essential states of human emotion, or *rasas*—eroticism or artfulness, humor, compassion, fierceness, heroism, fearfulness, disgust, wonder, and peacefulness. Children should be allowed free expression of all nine rasas. Authoritarian discipline or too much fuss made about the rasas during childhood is seen as cause for stunted emotional growth and blockage of free self-expression as an adult. Yashoda's permissive attitude toward Krishna's naughtiness and childish pranks is the perfect illustration of this principle.

Above all, the story of Krishna's childhood tells us to let children be children—they are wonderful just the way they are.

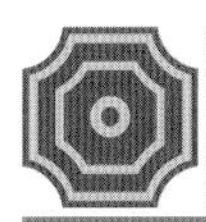

About the Illustrations

The original illustrations for *Little Krishna* are wash paintings done in both watercolors and opaque tempera paints. The artist created each piece following a nine-step traditional Indian process.

1. First, using watercolors, he drew the outlines of everything in the painting.
2. Before filling in the outlines he had to fix the line drawing by pouring water over the painted surface until only the paint absorbed by the paper remained.
3. Once the painting was completely dry, he filled in all the forms with color, using three tones for each color to achieve a three-dimensional effect: highlight, middle tone, and depth.
4. Once again the colors had to be fixed by pouring water over the painting until it ran off clear.
5. Then, still using watercolor, he applied the background colors, shading the background to a darker tone in the corners of the painting.
6. Once again the colors had to be fixed.
7. Then the artist was ready to apply the wash, which is done with opaque tempera paints mixed to a consistency between thin honey and boiled milk. Before applying the wash, he had to wet the painting thoroughly, letting any excess water drip off. Then he applied the tempera paint until the whole painting appeared to be behind a colored fog. While the wash color was still wet, he took a dry brush and removed it from the face, hands, and feet of any figures. Then he let the wash dry completely.
8. Once again water had to be poured over the entire painting to fix the color. Many of the paintings received several washes and fixes before the right color tone was achieved. The wash color is important because it sets the emotional mood of the whole painting.
9. Finally, the artist went back in and redefined the delicate line work of the piece, outlining faces, fingers, toes, and ornaments with the depth color. These finishing touches allow the painting to reemerge from within the clouds of wash.

To give children an opportunity for hands-on participation in this ancient art form, we have included a line drawing of Krishna on the following page. Feel free to trace or photocopy the image so that children may color it in.

ॐ नमो भगवते वासुदेवाय ॐ नमो भगवते वासुदेवाय